Arthur Wooten's Shorts

STROKE OF LUCK
a short story
&
The *"Dear Henry"* Letters

ARTHUR WOOTEN

GALAXIAS PRODUCTIONS

Arthur Wooten's Shorts
STROKE OF LUCK
a short story
&

The *"Dear Henry"* Letters

Galaxias Productions
200 West 90th Street Suite 9B
New York, NY 10024

All rights reserved.

ISBN: 978-0-9835631-9-8

Graphic Art by: Bud Santora

DEDICATION

To all the shorts out there that have ever
felt intimidated by the novels.
Stand tall!

CONTENTS

STROKE OF LUCK

a short story

"Don't be shy, Billy," I whispered. "Bend over sexy and open it up."

He looked back at me with a sly grin. "Should I arch my back?"

"We have to turn this up a notch," I said laughing as I punched in 375 degrees on my computerized Presidential professional oven. "Now I want you to grab hold of my baster and gently squeeze the knob so that my delicious juices squirt all over that chicken."

And chicken Billy was. Who knew that at age fifty-one I'd be addicted to Wonder Bread and I'd have my pick of the loaf? And Billy, a dancer and wannabe actor, was definitely the favorite amongst my bevy of boys.

He basted the bird and then closed the oven. "I didn't know cooking could be so sexual."

I looked at my watch and then scooped him up into my arms. "I'll show you sexual."

1

I carried him out of the kitchen, through the dining room and into the bedroom of my New York City apartment. At five-foot-eight and weighing one hundred and sixty pounds, Billy was the perfect fit for me. I like guys a bit smaller. It keeps me on top of my game, if you know what I mean.

"My God you are *the* hunk," Billy said looking up into my pale blue eyes. "I'd better be careful or I could..."

I cut him off. "Don't say it. We've talked about this before."

"I've just never met anyone like you and I know you have other boys but I..."

I threw him onto my bed, planted my lips onto his and kissed him quickly to shift his train of thought. I heard him moan as he surrendered to my touch and like any one of my signature dishes, I ate up every morsel of him, from head to toe. I take great pride in satisfying people's hunger, both gastronomically and sexually. I think they go hand in hand.

After our big quickie, I checked my watch as Billy jumped into the shower. By the time he was dried off and wearing one of my bathrobes I had dinner plated and wine poured.

Billy sat down at the table and looked at the feast before him. "You feed me too well, Chip Lowell. In more ways than one."

We clinked glasses.

I pondered. "What should we toast to?"

Billy didn't hesitate for a moment. "Here's to *City Cooking, Country Boy*, and an Emmy."

"From your mouth to voter's ears!"

I had recently landed my own television cooking show.

2

The day before, we had finished the pilot episode and the buzz in the industry was fantastic. I had come into my own. But trust me, I had paid my dues. After slaving away for years in restaurants, first starting out as a busboy and then a waiter, I got on-the-job training and eventually worked my way up from sous chef to executive chef at one of Manhattan's most prominent French restaurants. After securing my celebrity chefhood, I was courted by other restaurant owners and encouraged to jump ship. Several even offered to open up my own place. But the best offer of all came when the program director of The Eats Network discovered me and thought I had the potential to be their next superstar. We shot an audition tape and considering I live in the Big Apple but grew up on a farm in New England, it made perfect sense to call my show, *City Cooking, Country Boy.*

In no time at all, both Billy and I had devoured our simple but tasty dinner.

He winked at me. "What's for dessert?"

"You asked for it, kiddo."

I jumped up from the table and surprisingly he did too. He may have been small, but Billy was fast. I chased him all over the apartment and finally corned him against the back of the over-sized leather sofa in front of my west-facing wall of windows. Recently I had purchased this 14th floor, loft-like dwelling, which was located in an ultra modern building built on the corner of Jane and West Streets.

I tore open his bathrobe and started devouring Billy all over again. How could his skin feel so soft and taste so fresh? Maybe because he was only twenty-two? Honestly, I had never been into young guys before, it's just that after I turned fifty, they started flinging themselves at me. My mouth and hands were everywhere.

"Stop, Chip," Billy squealed. "What if someone sees us?"

"Then lucky them," I laughed. "Besides, we're facing the Hudson River. They'd either have to be in a helicopter or looking through a gigantic telescope aimed at us from Jersey."

I've never been this horny in my life. And once we were both sated, I pulled myself off of Billy and he literally fell asleep on the couch. I looked at my watch, jumped into the shower and then went into my bedroom.

Eventually Billy walked in and saw his clothes laid out on my bed. "I hate it when you do that."

I was sitting at my computer returning emails as I looked up at him. "Would you rather I say, 'Please leave now?'"

"It's just so obvious." Billy reluctantly put his clothes back on. "Why won't you ever let me spend the night?"

"Because I have to be up at the crack of dawn and I need my sleep. I have an onsite food demo I have to do at The Chelsea Food Market tomorrow for the press to promote the show and I'm still working on the script."

"It's always career for you."

I stood up and put my arms around him. "It is right now, kiddo."

* * *

Up at 5:30AM the next morning, I jogged to my gym, did a light weight lifting routine and climbed the rock wall. I love sports. All sports. In high school I was quarterback

4

for our football team in fall, ran the relay and did the long jump for indoor track in winter and played shortstop for the baseball team in spring. Once I was in college I enjoyed skiing, both snow and water, mountain climbing, racquetball and tennis. Hey, I'm an all around jock.

After my workout I opted for a quick thirty-minute massage. I would have encouraged the practitioner to go beyond the call of duty and give me the release I could tell he was aching to offer but time was short and instead, I gave him a nice big tip.

I thank my parents for the great genes I've inherited and coupled with my healthy eating and vigorous lifestyle, I must admit, I've preserved myself pretty well. Most guess I'm at least ten years younger than I am. And some may call me cocky, others obnoxious. I'm just self-confident and it's gotten me to where I am today. I love my fucking life.

As I headed out of the gym, the bright sunlight as it always does, triggered off a sneeze. It may sound weird but I enjoy sneezing. I like the sensation of it. And I'm fascinating with the fact that colds don't make me sneeze, allergies don't make me sneeze, just bright light. Go figure.

I hailed a cab and shot up to 15th Street and 9th Avenue. I ran my hand over my carefully shaven head and checked to make sure that I had thrown my clean white chef's coat into my garment bag. It was an exceptionally warm September day and although it was still early, the market was teeming with people upon my arrival.

The Chelsea Market was once the Nabisco Cookie Factory where the Oreo was invented. But after being left abandoned for years, the warehouse was transformed into an upscale city mall offering more than twenty specialty shops ranging from kitchen supplies to flowers to exotic foods, spices, desserts and wines. They also offer food tastings, live concerts and today…moi!

From the moment I signed on the dotted line I felt like I was at home with The Eats Network. From the president and CEO to my stage manager and food assistants, I was in heaven. This was one organized organization.

My food station was all set up for the demo. A combination of city and country décor, it reflected the approach to my show. Constructed around my cook station was a semi-round table set for eight people. Included would be food critics from *TV Guide, Gourmet, Bon Appetit, Country Living, Food and Wine, Southern Living* and *Good Housekeeping.* But in my mind, just as important as the industry bigwigs, so were the shoppers mulling around the market. In truth, they would make up more of my audience than the critics.

After a quick run through of the three course meal I was going to prepare and making sure everything was in place, I dashed upstairs to a rented space next to the Oxygen Network offices. I dropped to the floor, did fifty push-ups, slipped on my crisp white chef's coat with my name and the show's monogrammed onto it and then had make-up shine me down. The Eats Network was also filming the event to use for future promos.

Excited to say the least, I headed back downstairs where my producer Paul Connor rushed to my side.

"Hey big guy," he said shaking my hand. "This is the beginning of a long and beautiful relationship."

"The feeling's mutual, Paul." I checked out the scores of people gathered around my set. In the back of the

6

crowd I was actually surprised to see Billy. Catching his eye, I threw him a wink. And then it was showtime.

Paul introduced me to the crowd, there was a round of applause and I stepped up to my cook station and into the bright lights.

"Thank you for joining me today. My name is Chip Lowell and welcome to my show *City Cooking, Country Boy.*"

There was more applause and I started in with the concept of the show.

"I'm just a country boy living in the big city. I want to share with you the comfort of good old fashioned home cooking with the speed, ease and healthiness that today's lifestyle calls for."

There was another round of applause.

"On today's menu we have a three green salad with a champagne vinaigrette topped with edible and peppery nasturtium flowers. We also have my grandma's brilliant shepherd's pie with her secret ingredient of cabbage and caraway seeds. And for dessert, well, I'm going to let that be a surprise."

As I started prepping the salad I wanted to warm up to the crowd and critics with a personal story.

"In my family, everyone loved to cook. And because I'm an only child and my grandparents and parents have all since passed, cooking for me, especially recipes we shared together, keeps them close to my heart."

I heard a collective emotional sigh from the group when suddenly, a bright studio light, popped on overhead. Not surprisingly, I felt a sneeze coming on but not wanting to spray germs all over my food, I turned away from the counter and held the sneeze in making a ridiculously high squeaking sound. I smiled, turned back to the eager crowd and then felt an odd pressure surge down both my arms.

"Well, that sneeze was not on the menu," I said while quickly washing my hands.

The crowd laughed as I regrouped.

"As I thaw slaying." I stopped, hearing myself. I was thinking the right words, they just didn't come out. I tried again. "Af a vaw fray..." Suddenly, white dots appeared in my vision and then everything went black.

* * *

When I came to, I saw Paul and a paramedic standing over me. I was being strapped into a gurney and tried to ask what was going on, but my words were all distorted. The crowd made way for them to wheel me out of the market and Paul was allowed to ride in the ambulance with me. The last face I saw as they closed the back of the ambulance door was Billy's. He looked so frightened.

In the ambulance I heard discussion as to whether or not I should be taken right to St. Lucia's Hospital or down to Maxwell Radiology for an MRI. It was obvious that time was of the essence so it was off to St. Lucia's for a CAT scan.

I've never been hospitalized a day in my life and considering the whirlwind of activity I didn't even have time to be frightened or upset. In fact, my brain felt foggy, like everything was on hold. Upon arriving at St. Lucia's I was rushed into the CAT scan room, locked in place under the x-ray tunnel and they started computerizing my brain as fast as they could. I remember a dye being in-

8

jected into my arm and then the rest was blank.

I woke up in a hospital room. No one was there. I was connected to an IV and some sort of monitoring system. I could just barely move my right arm and leg. The left side of my body felt dead. I tried to speak and gibberish came out. Just then a zaftig Latino entered the room.

"Hey Chip, welcome back," he said smiling. "My name is Allie." He pressed a call button and then came over to my side.

When I struggled to talk, he shook his head. "Rest. No matter how hard you try right now, it's not going to come out right. Talk about drama. Nothing like having a stroke while on television."

A stroke? I had a stroke? But that's impossible. I'm healthy as a horse. There's no history of it in my family. I'm only fifty-one!

"I know what you're thinking but anybody can have one at anytime. You're going to be OK."

A disheveled looking doctor entered the room.

"Mr. Lowell, I'm Dr. Laytner. How are you feeling?"

I wanted to say that I had to get back to the live demo but what came out was unintelligible.

The doctor touched my arm. "I can see that you're having some trouble speaking."

You bet the hell I am! Give me something and let me get back to work!

He continued while looking at my charts. "The bad news is, you had an ischemic stroke. A blood clot blocked a blood vessel in your brain and we're already treating you with a drug called t-PA. It dissolves the clot. The good news is, every minute counts when someone is having a stroke and they got you here pretty quickly."

9

A generic looking nurse entered and fiddled with the IV.

"Chip," Dr. Laytner explained, "although stroke is a disease of the brain, it can affect the entire body. The effects can range from mild to severe and can include paralysis, problems with thinking, speaking and emotional outbursts. Patients may also experience pain or numbness after a stroke. Time will tell. I'm hoping that with your strong body, determination and the help of your occupational therapist, Allie, and the rest of our team, we'll keep symptoms to a minimum."

A minimum? I have a fucking television show to do!

"We'll watch you closely and put you through so much testing that you'll want to run out of here." The doctor laughed at his own bad joke. "And hopefully you will. Allie will work with you and help re-teach you how to feed yourself, get dressed, bathe...all the day-to-day stuff that we take for granted."

Just my luck to get an overweight Hispanic who was probably in his late thirties to sponge bathe me every day.

"Hey buddy," Paul whispered as he walked gingerly into the room.

I tried to smile, I tried to sit up, I tried to talk...but I couldn't.

"Just relax. All is good. Of course the show will be put on hold but not to worry."

I tried to talk again.

"And financially, insurance is taking care of everything. Hey buddy, gotta run. A lot of fires to put out. See you soon?"

And then he started out the door. I wanted to scream at him and order him to stay and help me and tell me more. But he left.

Dr. Laytner looked at his watch. "I'll check in with you later Chip. You don't have high blood pressure, heart disease, diabetes or high cholesterol. We even checked to see if there's a hole in your heart. Sometimes a piece of plaque can escape that way but yours is perfect. My suggestion to you is, never ever hold a sneeze in again." He smiled at me. "Hey, you know why you close your eyes instinctually when you sneeze? Cause they'll pop out." He laughed and left with the nurse.

Allie looked over at me. "It's true."

What nightmare was I in and how do I get out of it? How long do I lie here? When can I speak? Or walk?

There was a knock at the door and Billy popped his head in. "All right if I say hello?"

I tried to smile but sensed my face was lopsided.

Allie got up out of his chair. "Chip's a bit tongue tied."

Billy walked in and stood next to me, at least an arm's length away from the bed.

"Hey big guy," he said nervously. "Wow, you gave quite a show."

I tried to tell him with my eyes how grateful I was, not only that he had shown up at the demo but also that he had followed me to the hospital.

"I just had a quick lesson in how life can throw you a curve ball," he laughed nervously.

You did! How about me?

"Listen, I'm going to come back every day and stay as long as you like and keep you company. I'm sure you'll be out of here in no time and back on the show before you know it." Billy looked at his watch. "I have to head off to a dance class and then I have an audition at 4:00PM. I'll

11

drop by after?"

I struggled to nod my head and then weakly waved my right hand. He smiled but didn't touch me. And then he left. Billy never came back.

* * *

I was in St. Lucia's for almost a month and in that time my muscles atrophied and I lost fifteen pounds. Paul visited me once more. No one else dropped by. No one. My doctors zoomed in and out and the nurses were pleasant enough but it was Allie whom I spent most of my days with. I confess that he had really grown on me and as pathetic as it sounds, he was the only friend I had.

When I wasn't being tortured in physical therapy, I wasted way too many hours watching shitty television and tried hopelessly to concentrate on a novel. Every day Allie read the newspapers to me and I discovered that he had a wicked sense of humor. He also told me that his full name was Alejandro del Valle and I was impressed to find out that he was actually fifty-three. Although chunky, he was doing something right.

With rehabilitation therapy I had gained back some use of my left arm and left leg. I was actually capable of walking short distances on my own but after a few feet I was completely exhausted. And my speech was slow but much improved. Two of my biggest challenges were undressing and bathing.

Allie turned on the shower as I struggled to get my boxers off of my left leg.

"Get your ass in here, Lowell."

I sat on the edge of the bed. "These fucking bloomers

you have me wearing get caught on my left foot."

He stuck his head out of the bathroom. "I told you, I'm not helping you with that anymore, you can do it on your own. Just lift your left foot with your right hand."

I did and managed to untangle myself.

"Now march yourself in here, private," Allie ordered.

With all my strength, I got to a standing position as he watched. "You just want to get a great big look at my dick," I said playing with him.

"Oh, please! I've seen so many of those little things in my day."

I grabbed hold of my walker and made it to the bathroom door. As I struggled to get through the door I unexpectedly brushed against Allie's body with my butt and suddenly I was erect. I was actually stunned at my reaction. Embarrassed, I turned away from him but the shower water was a little too hot so I twisted back in his direction.

"Mmmm, and I see your private is at attention, also."

I turned away feeling like a hormonal teenager as it got harder.

"Hey, Lowell, this will help."

Allie walked towards me with his hand outstretched. I thought he was going to grab it, which in turn made it throb but instead he shut off the hot water, showering me with cold. I screamed as he left the bathroom laughing.

"I have to run down to administration, Chip. I'll be back in bit," Allie hollered.

I adjusted the temperature and had to quickly jerk-off. After cleaning up I carefully made my way back into the room and laughed so hard when I saw my bed. Allie had laid out my clothing just like I had for Billy. This truly was my biggest challenge, getting dressed. I managed to get everything on, except for my shirt, by the time Allie got back.

"I'm sorry I missed you taking care of your little friend," Allie snickered as he walked back in.

I gave him a devilish grin. "You'd better be careful of what you ask for."

I lifted my left arm with my right and he slipped my left hand through the sleeve of my shirt.

"You know Allie, upon discharge I need a full time professional to live with me."

He adjusted my shirt and started buttoning it. "Yes, I know."

I felt a bit awkward asking him but I thought I'd give it a shot. "I know they are going to assign someone, but would you be willing or even capable of moving in with me for a while, till I get my feet back on the ground?"

Allie smiled. "That was a bad pun. I'd have to get clearance through my boss. But why me?"

"Well, I've gotten used to you?"

He stopped with the buttons, took a step back and stared at me. "Thanks man," he said sardonically. "It's nice to be used to."

"You know what I mean." I felt bad the way that came out. "You're great at what you do and I like you but I didn't know if you had someone you were close to that would mind if you were gone at night."

"You're fishing and I'm single."

"Oh, OK. Where do you live?"

He put my loafers in front of me. "After weeks of practically living with me *now* you want the personal details? The Bronx. I'd tell you what street but I'm sure you've

14

never heard of it."

"I'm sure, too." I slipped the right one on easily.

"Have you ever been to the Bronx?"

Allie wrestled to get my left shoe on my foot.

"Of course."

"You lie!"

"I drive, or I used to drive through the Bronx all the time, very quickly, to get to Westchester."

We both laughed.

* * *

Allie definitely felt the wow factor as he wheeled me into my loft.

"Welcome to my digs," I said as I rolled over to my plants. "I can't believe they're all dead."

He put his suitcase down and went over to a window to let in some fresh air. "These are all cactuses. They shouldn't have died in the time you were gone?"

"Uh, well they were dead before then."

Allie gave me a sarcastic look.

I spun around in the chair. "But now what?"

Allie checked out my state of the art kitchen. "Now what, what?"

I threw my good arm up into the air. "I mean what the fuck do I do now?"

"I think you congratulate yourself."

I wheeled over to him. "For what?"

"In the beginning you were frightened, then you were depressed and now you're angry. And that's good. Healthy. Progress."

Hell, I was always angry.

15

Allie picked up his bag and walked down the hallway. "Where's my room?"

I chased him with my chair. "To your left."

He threw his suitcase on the bed and started opening it. "First, I check out your apartment. Then, what we do are daily things. Like vacuuming, washing clothes..."

"I have a freaking housekeeper that does that. I want to go to the gym. I want to run a mile. I want to climb a mountain." I struggled to get up out of the chair and to a standing position. "I want to cook. I want to do my TV show. I want to be me, again!"

I was very unsteady and aimed my body for the bed but misjudged, hit the side of it, bounced off and landed on the hard floor. Shockingly, I of all people, started to cry.

Allie got down on the floor next to me and rolled me onto my back. I couldn't stop the tears. He sat above me and laid my head in his lap.

"Just let out," he whispered, quietly.

"It's all just so...shocking. It's fucking shocking. I mean I know I'm doing well but I still can't believe this has happened to me. My life was all planned out. I was just about to make it big and..."

I slowly quieted down as Allie gently massaged my forehead. A few minutes must have passed by when I looked up at him. His eyes were closed and he seemed to be in a meditative trance.

Suddenly he said very sweetly, "Shit happens."

It sounded so inappropriate yet so perfect that I started to laugh. Then he started to laugh.

"Allie, you know what I want?"

"What's that?"

I rolled myself onto my strong right elbow. "Food. Good food. Any kind of food but hospital food."

* * *

From my wheelchair I tried to hover around Allie once he got back from the store and watched him take items out of the bags. Among the many things I could see that he had bought oregano, garlic, cumin and bay laurel leaves.

"I have most of these ingredients here."

"And you've been away for weeks. I want fresh!" Allie exclaimed.

"This is all wrong. I told you what to get."

He looked me straight in the eye. "No, you ordered me what to get. And considering I'm making dinner, I'll choose the ingredients."

I sat there with my mouth open. "Who's making dinner?"

He looked me up and down. "I don't think *you* are."

I checked out all the ingredients. "Black beans, jalapeños, jicama? What are you, Puerto Rican?"

"¡Pido su perdón!" Allie exclaimed indignantly. "¡Soy Cubano!"

"Cuban? But you have sandy blonde hair and green eyes."

"And everyone from Cuba has to look like Ricky Ricardo? Go make yourself useful and mix us up a couple of cocktails."

"So bossy," I said under my breath.

"And thank you for noticing the color of my eyes," Allie said winking at me.

"You're welcome."

"And I bought some mint so you can make us Moji-tos." Allie looked over at me. "You do know how to make a Mojito, don't you?"

"Yes," I boasted. "I know how to make a Mojito."

I think I do. I wheeled into my bedroom and to the computer to quickly look up a recipe for the drink when I heard him holler from the kitchen.

"Save yourself some time. It's three parts rum, one part lime juice, two teaspoons of sugar, four mint leaves, dash of soda."

I came out my bedroom with my tail between my legs. "You're a mind reader."

"I knew you were going to say that."

* * *

It felt so odd not to be the one cooking, especially in my own kitchen. But considering how strong I made the Mo-jitos and it being my first drink in weeks, it actually was enjoyable to let someone else take care of things.

"It's all ready," Allie said as he started to serve the meal.

I wheeled over and lit the candles on the dining room table as he brought over the dishes. "Allie, I'm sorry that I don't have a Cuban wine, but I did open a Chilean Char-donnay."

"Good. Cuban wines suck."

I struggled to get out of the wheelchair and onto the dining room chair. And I like the fact that he could have helped me but sensed I wanted to do it on my own. "This meal really smells delicious."

"My abuela's recipe for spicy mojo chicken with black

beans and mandarin oranges."

I went through my broken Spanish. "Grandmother?"

He nodded as we started eating. "I was raised by her. In the early 50s my grandfather died and she immigrated to the States. My mother and father were going to join her but stayed in Cuba a bit too long. Unfortunately, Castro appeared. I was their only child and born with a congenital heart disorder that needed complicated surgery and just by luck of the draw, I was allowed to leave Cuba and was flown to New York."

"Damn, that's tough, being a little kid and all."

"The operation was a success and my family knowing I would have a better life here, encouraged me to stay on with my abuela in the Bronx. I was really close to her, but she is gone now."

I smiled at him. "You know, the day...*it* happened...I was preparing my late abuela's recipe, shepherd's pie."

We held up wine glasses and toasted, "To our abuelas."

* * *

It tasted so good and not just because it wasn't hospital food. We gobbled up each and every little bite.

"Allie, you are a wonderful cook."

He actually blushed which I found very endearing.

"That is a real compliment, Chip, coming from you."

"Someday you'll make someone a great husband."

"Actually I did, once," he said, rather flippantly. "But he's history."

"Left you for another guy, huh?" I asked teasing him.

"No, he died." He got up from the table and took our

plates into the kitchen.

I was mortifyingly embarrassed. "I'm so sorry."

"Don't worry about it. Like I said, shit happens. I met a great guy, loved him for almost ten years and then he got cancer." He came back and poured more wine into our glasses. "But that was quite a while ago. Chip, why don't you go over to the sofa and I'll bring the dessert?"

I sensed he wanted to change the subject. I managed very carefully to stand up and while walking over there I rested against a chest in front of my large mirror.

"Jesus, the left side of my face still looks like it's melted."

"Maybe if you have an overdose of Botox on the right side, it will even out," Allie shouted from the kitchen.

I smiled as I barely made it to the sofa. Allie brought over two ramekins full of flan, two spoons and set them down on the coffee table.

"Now these I did not make myself, as you know."

He dashed back to the dining room table, brought over the wine and our glasses and plopped himself down on the couch.

I studied him. "You have beautiful skin."

I realized this made him uncomfortable as we each took a sip of our wine.

He gently brushed his hand along his forearm. "Don't be silly."

I looked at him seriously. "I really mean it. You have beautiful olive skin."

Allie eventually broke the awkward silence. "And I think you're much more attractive now then when you entered the hospital."

I almost choked on my wine. "I what?"

Allie laughed. "You were all puffed up like a blowfish."

"I wasn't puffed up, I was muscular."

"And insecure."

I frowned at him. I had to think about that one.

"But Chip, talk about insecure? I'm shocked that your little friend never came back to see you."

"Billy," I said almost under my breath.

"When a crisis like this happens in your life, you realize who your real friends are."

"Or if you had any to begin with." We both sipped our wines in silence. "You seem to be somewhat of a loner, too."

Allie eyed me suspiciously. "I guess I've never looked at it like that before. I have acquaintances but actually, my work fills up the social void in my life."

"Are your parents still in Cuba?"

It was obvious that I pushed an emotional button. I put my glass down and touched his arm. "I'm sorry, I didn't mean to intrude."

"You're not intruding, I already brought them up. It's just that I haven't talked about them in a long time." He took a deep breath. "My father was an outspoken journalist against Castro and his Communist regime and was eventually imprisoned. I think he must have died in jail sometime in the late 70s because in 1981 my mother boarded a small boat in an attempt to flee to Miami. Overcrowded and with no life preservers, it capsized during a storm and all were lost at sea. I was so young when I moved up here that I don't remember my parents at all. It's like they never existed."

He looked so sad it broke my heart. "I'm sorry, Allie."

He slowly turned towards me and smiled. I leaned in

21

and our mouths almost touched. I took a chance, kissed him lightly on the lips and then he pulled away. A moment passed and then he slid his forearm behind my neck, pulled me to him and kissed me with fiery passion. It's hard to explain, but something clicked inside of me, like that last number you're fumbling for that opens up a lock. As odd as it felt intellectually, my heart knew I had met a kindred soul. I kissed him deeper and we fell into one another.

When we finally parted lips, we looked into each other's eyes and then burst out into laughter. Not laughter like this was such as stupid thing to do, but laughter because it took both of us so long to find this.

Without speaking, Alejandro del Valle stood up and reached out for my hands. With all my might, I made it to a standing position and then without any warning, he scooped me up into his arms. Life had come full circle. I was now the man being swept off my feet.

But, Allie made it about three steps and thank God we were still next to the sofa because he didn't have the strength to carry me and we both fell over, onto it.

"¡Dios querido del Oh!" Allie cried. "I think my back went out."

He helped me to my feet and together we supported each other, arm in arm, back to my bedroom.

Who knew that a chubby, middle-aged Cuban with blonde hair, green eyes and olive skin would turn out to be the sexiest and kindest man I have ever kissed in my life?

The

"Dear Henry"

Letters

(About The Letters)

For two years, from March of 2008 to April of 2010, Arthur was the humorist for the London magazine, **reFRESH**. The publishers wanted him to write about gay sex, love, dating, and fetishes but instead of it being the typical advice column, Arthur came up with a creative way to address the challenges of courting in the 21st century.

In each issue of this beautiful and glossy oversized gay publication, he wrote a letter to his exasperating and fictional lover, Henry, explaining the never-ending reasons why they must end their relationship.

But as we all know, sometimes breaking up can be *really* hard to do.

LET'S CALL IT SPLITS

March/April 2008

Dear Henry,

It pains me to have to write this letter but you've given me no choice. It hurts so much because I bent over backwards...and forwards for that matter...and yet you never gave me an inch. I'm sorry, that's not true. You almost gave me 5.5 inches but I didn't penalize you for that.

You have to admit, our initial meeting was like a fairy tale. If you recall, we romantically met in a chat room online. I told you that I was a former gymnast, kind of average looking, a successful writer and somewhere between 31 and death. And you told me how tall, dark and handsome you were and that you were 38 and then we exchanged pictures.

But I didn't hold it against you when we met in person at that charming café and you ordered a coke and vodka and discovered you were short, light and a bit quirky looking. And the fact that you were older than you said didn't faze me at all. With Internet age, you always add on an extra five years. But I was a bit surprised when I realised the photo you sent me was not your picture. Heck, I've only seen one Colin Farrell movie so I thought it could have been you. Call me madcap, but I think that was bit deceitful.

One must admit though we both felt a lot of chemistry

right away and at the end of that first date I'm glad we didn't jump right into bed. It felt mature that we took our time getting to know one another and held off on having sex. To give in to lust and temptation would have felt cheap and easy. I'm glad we waited till the second date.

Some may have thought that your food eccentricities might be a turn off but not me. I have never met anyone before who would only eat white food. But as long as you're getting all your nutrients, why not? White rice, white cheese, white milk, white cauliflower, white beans, white bread, boiled chicken. (But the chicken did look a bit more grey than white.) That's a hard food group to work with. I'm proud of the surprise dinner I came up with but am sorry that some parsley landed on your plate and ruined the meal for you.

And did I judge you when we visited my friend Jon's house in the country for the weekend and you brought along your formal wear? If you find standing in the middle of his pool, soaking wet in an Armani suit hot and sexy, I say, "Go for it." Although, you might want to be a bit more practical and invest in less expensive suits. One dunk and it's ruined. We all know that you telemarketers don't make a lot of money.

And didn't you say when we first met that you were versatile? If you are, you're doing it with someone other than me. You're not a top. You're not a bottom. You're a side. I was willing to meet you half way but instead you made me do all the work. I can see your face right now. You're making that combination condescending smirk slash frown. I'm not being critical, just honest.

But I worked through all of that and I know that relationships take time and patience and sometimes compromise. So when you asked me if I was into leather, something that's never been on my sexual "to do" list, I thought to myself, "Be open. Why not give it a try? Especially if it will make him happy." I actually started having visions of leather harnesses, biker jackets and even hooded masks. Just the thought of the smell of leather was beginning to turn me on.

Hence, the night we planned our fetish adventure I was completely psyched and ready to explore new worlds and facets of my sexual being. And to experience it for the first time with you meant so much to me. But I was at a total loss when you showed up at my place empty handed and then went rummaging through my closet. And what did you pull out? A pair of dusty leather tassel loafers.

The devilish look on your face when you discovered them, the glimmer in your eye, the heavy breathing was all quite confusing not to mention disturbing. I remember you brought the shoes over to me and asked, "Are you passionate about slip-ons?" And I thought to myself, "A slip-on dildo maybe, but an old shoe?" You were practically drooling over that pigskin and honestly it was uncomfortable for me to watch you sodomise them. I had to leave the bedroom so you and the pair could finish your business. I've heard of threesomes but this was ridiculous. And I'll never forget what you screamed at me from the bedroom.

"You're jealous Arthur, aren't you?"

I may be guilty of being jealous of other people's money, careers or even looks but I'm not jealous of my own pair of shoes. By the way, you ruined the leather. I think it's only fair that you financially compensate me for it.

Henry, I think it's best if we part ways. When in relationships, whether they be with family, friends or loved ones, we all must be adaptable. How can you ask me to be free as the wind and go with the flow when you yourself are so stiff and rigid? Actually, it would have been nice if you did get stiff and rigid. But I'm not one to hold grudges.

And in life, we constantly have to switch gears. Just remember to use the clutch. And stay flexible. Hell, I can still do my splits. Can you?

All the best,
Arthur

DON'T IT MAKE MY BROWN EYE, BLUE

May/June 2008

Dear Henry,

I'm intrigued, if not confused, that we are still together.
But I understand that relationships on any level take an
element of give and take. On that note, I feel like I've
been taking a lot more than giving. In fact, every time we
have sex now, you're the pitcher and I'm the catcher. Not
that I'm counting, but I would like to be on top of my
game, once in a while.

And I was so impressed that you listened to what I
had to say in my last letter,

"...in life, we constantly have to switch gears. Just remember to use the clutch."

But I meant it figuratively, not literally. So when the
rusted out 1998 Allegro convertible with the tear in the
roof that is patched with electrician's tape appeared in
front of my house with a big bow on it and a note saying,
"To Arthur, Enjoy my stick shift, Henry," I was quite
overwhelmed to say the least. Especially since I don't
drive. I thought Allegro was an opera. Or maybe an anti-
histamine? I hope you didn't actually pay money for that
car. You have your self-esteem to think of. And could you
please remove it? The car, that is. It's illegally parked,

piled high with violation tickets and there's a large but pretty yellow device attached to the back wheel.

However, Henry, I must confess I have enjoyed your "joy stick". There's something very comfortable about small penises. But I know you're frustrated with my inability to understand how to work with your hood — and I'm not referring to the Allegro. You blame it on the fact that I'm cut. I wish I wasn't. Or at the very least, I should have had a say in the decision process. I want it back.

So I girded my loins, took a deep breath and allowed you to attach that non-surgical foreskin restoration device to my talliwacker. The metal clamp was a bit tight and little cold but that was fine. What you didn't do was read the instructions carefully. It says it takes about one year to restore a man's foreskin, not one hour. Hence, it only makes sense that the extraordinary amount of weight that you attached to my shaft would have forced any man's skin that was left, to be violently torn off.

I'm sure you meant well so I'm not holding that against you. Besides, they say the stitches will dissolve on their own if infection doesn't set in. But it would be considerate if you helped out with the price—insurance isn't covering it. Oh, and when the weight hit my foot, the doctor said they just let broken toes heal on their own.

Lightheaded from the painkillers, I limped to a friend's house who reminded me that when it comes to relationships, compromise is imperative. So again, I let you have your way. I know you like a smooth hairless chest but why couldn't I have just shaved it off? Yes, when it grows back it becomes very stubbly, but exfoliation, especially for your face Henry, would be a good thing.

29

But I acquiesced and allowed you to use the home wax method. Before you came over that night I was really excited. Knowing my man was going to groom my body the way he wanted it and then ravage me seemed so erotic. I understand that hot wax removal dates back to the ancient Egyptians and even Alexander The Great had his body parts done to keep looking youthful and sexy. Now that's hot! And so was the paraffin wax you boiled up. But burns heal and you did yank the cloth strips at the proper 40-degree angle and yes it did remove my hair but unfortunately part of my areola came off with it, too. Not to worry. They grafted skin from the inside of my cheek onto my nipple and although the left side is obviously larger now then the right, it is smooth. You got your wish. They said hair will never grow there again.

I thought it only fair at this stage of the game to bring up a point of contention. Several rather sharp points. I'm not criticising your dental hygiene or lack thereof but those canines of yours are lethal. I've heard that lots of orally challenged men wear mouth guards when going down on their partners. It's rather like being gummed to death. But is it my fault that your lower guard popped loose and lodged in your throat? Lucky for you I know the Heimlich maneuver.

I give you 'A' for effort. And speaking of 'A's' I appreciate the article you shared with me from that New York magazine that exclaimed – "Anal Bleaching! It's All The Rage!" The cream you sent over was very effective but I don't think the added sun block was necessary. I read the instructions and applied it just as they told me to and then it said I should see gradual results quickly. That should have been the tip off for me. Gradual results quickly? While imitating Michael Jackson singing "A, B, C, easy as 1, 2, 3..." the bleaching cream morphed into battery acid and I couldn't wipe it off fast enough. With tears of pain streaming down my face I was able to make out on the back of the jar the word "CAUTION" in tiny little print. "This product contains 20% hydroquinone, a suspected carcinogen banned by several countries including the UK."

"Anal Bleaching! It's All The Rage!" Yeah, it's a real scream. Henry, I've given and taken as much as I can handle. It's over. I wish you well but I must insist that we not see each other again.

I've worked hard for my brown eye and I intend on keeping it. And if I get bum cancer, it's your ass that's on the line!

All the best,
Arthur

AND THIS LITTLE PIGGY...

July/August 2008

Dear Henry,

You never cease to amaze me.

After I expressed to you in my previous letter the pain and fear I endured when applying your anal bleaching cream to a certain private part of my body, to show your apologies and concern you went out and did the most romantic thing. You got a tattoo. But not just any tattoo you'd find on an arm, chest or a leg. No, you chose the image of an extremely large bull's-eye with multi-colours and had it excruciatingly tattooed onto your exceptionally small bum with the epicenter guiding me right to your point of entry. (I guess in case I got lost?) And above that you had my name written as a tramp stamp. I'm never going to judge a gay man by his cover, again.

I was moved to tears as I'm sure you were too while they were soldering the indelible ink into your body. But Henry, you spelled my name wrong. AUTHUR. You must have found a copy of my latest novel. My 'former' publishing house charmingly misspelled it that way, too. But I'm not a complainer; I'm a problem solver. So I was thinking you could try to turn the first 'u' into an 'r' but maybe it would be easier to change the second 'u' into an 'o'. AUTHOR. If you do that, it's probably best you keep having sex with writers from now on.

But what you did next totally baffled me. I know that body piercings are common even among children. We see it all the time. Ears, eyebrows, navels and noses. But why did you go out and get a Prince Albert? And then adorn it with the world's biggest and heaviest titanium circular barbell? I find it amusing that you have to sit down to pee because you're spraying all over the place and I understand you did it for me but dear Henry, I'll never go down on that thing. I'm not chipping a tooth.

Still, it is important in relationships to push one's limits and step outside of your comfort zone to keep things fresh and alive. So, when you suggested that I go out on the town with you and your so called A-list friends to help you forget about the fact that you've recently lost your job and run out of money, of course I said yes.

The hippest, hottest, most happening bar you dragged me to is one that I was at when it opened almost 15 years ago. But when we walked in, there were only five people there. Us. So you scurried me downstairs to the lounge. There we found a gaggle of boys barely of age all dressed in floss like g-strings ogling three men in jock straps who were being interviewed on a stage. I still say it makes sense that I thought they were playing the 'Dating Game'. How was I to know they were porno stars? And why were they so short?

I admit I was a bit uptight so I took you up on your offer to swallow a little something that you said would take the edge off of things but darling, that was not a sedative. Why are you and your friends taking mixed amphetamine salts? A drug prescribed for children with attention deficit disorder? It kept me up for 14 hours in a state of euphoria and I still haven't gotten my appetite back! Hmm, I should send some to my mother.

But I digress. After swallowing that bitter pill I was shocked to find out that you and your A-list gang of steroidal looking bodybuilders were all diabetics. I think. I'm sorry that I walked in on you in the men's room with each of you injecting each other in the butt. My bad.

After I made my way back to the stripper lounge and ordered another drink suddenly things got a little fuzzy. The stainless steel bar felt just like your Prince Albert and as I stroked it lovingly, I slipped and fell knocking down one metal stool after another, just like dominoes. Everyone looked over including the vertically challenged porno stars and then they all promptly ignored me. Stuck to something on the floor, it was the bartender who eventually came around to my rescue and asked, "Are you OK, Pops?" Pops!

Finally when it was time to leave and you asked if I'd engage in a 'spit-roast' I felt like I was in hog heaven. Who doesn't like a nice juicy slice of pork loin? You know I'm a huge foodie. What I didn't know is that it was going to be a threesome with you, your ex and me in the middle. Sorry, I'm not interested in that kind of sandwich.

Exhausted, I left the hippest, hottest, most happening bar alone and was horribly concerned when I couldn't reach you for days. You didn't answer your phone. You didn't answer your door. I was about to call the police when I realised they had called upon you. In today's paper there you were in all your glory. They had found you in the park hogtied from your genitals to your neck and buck-naked. They didn't name names but there was reference to a bull's-eye and the assumption that you were a writer who couldn't spell.

I may look a little conservative on the outside, but I'm just as piggy as the next guy on the inside. I'm sorry the authorities found certain illegal drugs stuffed into your clothes strewn about the bushes but now that you are incarcerated, I must think of my career and reputation. I can't date a convicted felon and I must turn down your offer for conjugal visits.

And it's imperative that we not see each other again.

Look at it this way Henry, jail is not a bad thing, especially for you. It's free rent, free food and I'm sure a lot free sex—whether you want it or not.

All the best,
Arthur

SPANX FOR THE MEMORY

September/October 2008

Dear Henry,

Once again, I'm stymied.

I was shocked but happy to hear that you were released from prison early due to good behavior and for having found religion. Scientology? They practice that in jail? I know you have to be gay to join but I thought the invitation into the cult was exclusively by knowing a certain A-list closeted Hollywood actor.

When I told my best friend of your release he encouraged me to forgive and forget and get back together with you. He said, "Yes Arthur, you are a homofessional gaylebrity but no one else is scratching at your door. All the guy did was get caught in the park naked and hog tied from his genitals to his neck and was under the influence of illegal drugs. Lighten up."

Oh hell, I forgive you and I'm proud that you've kicked your crystal meth habit. The least I could do was meet you at the outside gate as you left that nightmarish hellhole. But upon your exit, we turned around and saw hundreds of white handkerchiefs waving to you from cellblocks. And you shouted back, "I'll miss you Golof, I love you Jail Pussy and think of me One Eye!" I guess you made some new friends.

I had to ask you if Jail Pussy was what I thought it

was but you charmingly informed me that in the big house that's what you call men who have goatees. When I assumed that One Eye was another euphemism you corrected me and said that One Eye was Luther, your first cellmate.

"Arthur, one night while he was sleeping I gave him a prison eye patch."

"A what?" I asked cautiously.

"I teabagged his left eye. All the guys do it and unfortunately he got an infection and they had to remove it. His eye, that is. Feeling terribly guilty, the only thing I could offer him was my mind, body and soul for the rest of my stay."

That's awfully generous of you but Henry you've gained an enormous amount of weight. Standing 5' 8" tall you now weigh a whopping fifteen stone! You gained three in jail? I mean everyone comes out leaner. Robert Downey, Jr. is so hot at his prison weight and look how great Martha Stewart appeared after doing time. She was prison buff. What happened to you? I admit I'm a size queen, but this is ridiculous.

Henry, I thought I hit a nerve with the weight issue because you kept putting off us making love but when you confessed that you needed a little more time for an STD to clear up I thought that was very considerate. A little going away present from the inmates?

I was also surprised to see you wearing make-up. That was never your scene before being incarcerated. Nor is it mine. But I'm pushing myself to be more open-minded so if you want to paint the town and your face like Eddie Izzard, I support you 100 percent.

And to celebrate your newfound freedom I accepted

your invitation to meet you and a few of your friends at what you described as one of London's hottest clubs. Trannyshack? There were posters plastered all over the place that screamed Hot New Tranny Revue but you were nowhere to be found. So, I took a deep breath, entered Trannyshack and I don't think I exhaled until the show was over. I thought you were going to be with me watching the show, not starring in it.

Actually, you were quite entertaining as Chick Pee. You lost an amazing amount of weight in a very short period of time. And I had no idea you could lip synch. And to Azad's hip-hop theme song for the American television show Prison Break. You did it in German no less. Maybe you learned that in the slammer? Either way, I was impressed. And I liked your sidekicks, too. Hedda Romaine the tranny from Transylvania and the fire twirling circus drag queen Anita Light. Are they ex-convicts too?

So after your sold out and rocking opening show I was excited but nervous when you suggested we head back to my place to finally have sex. Nervous because I had now seen you as a woman. In truth, you looked just like my Aunt Loretta and I was desperately trying to erase that image from my mind. I watched you remove your humongous red wig, tear off your false eyelashes and then scrub your face clean.

Lying in my bed, I felt beads of sweat forming on my upper lip as you came to me still wearing your red sequined fishtail dress. Unfortunately, I was feeling more anxiety than lust. You turned your back, unzipped the gown and let it drop to the floor and that's when I gasped.

"What the hell is that?" I asked as I pointed to something you were wearing that made you look like a giant bratwurst.

You proudly shouted, "Spanx."

I shook my head. "You know I'm not into spanking."

"No Arthur, this is a Spanx. A body girdle. This style is called the Power Panty."

You had not lost a single dram! That human condom was so tight it was making your excess body fat roll up and over the top of the…Power Panty…making you look like you were wearing a huge muffin top just underneath your breasts.

Dear Henry, I patiently waiting for you to get out of jail, bided my time as you got rid of your VD, had my corneas irreparably scorched witnessing you as a drag queen and now I've seen your body revoltingly held together with the help of a woman's flesh squishing undergarment. I know prison is designed to change people but this is too much for me.

It's over. We're finished. Done. Finito. Auf Wiedersehen. I do forgive you but I can't forget. Goodbye, good luck and Spanx for the memory.

All the best,
Arthur

SOUND ADVICE

November/December 2008

Dear Henry,

In my last correspondence I said good-bye to you in as many different languages as I possibly could. And any normal person would have just told me to bugger off and gone on with their lives, but not you. Your response was, "My friends Todd and Glenn, who are a 'power gay' couple, have invited me to spend the weekend with them at their house by the sea. Walks on the beach. Fresh air. Warm fireplaces. Watching the stars from their terrace. Gourmet food. My advice is; rethink our relationship and please join me?"

I wasn't sure what 'power gay' meant, but it sounded like they had a lot of money so I had to say yes. (Sometimes my own shallowness frightens me.)

Instantly I had visions of us driving up to a Victorian architectural jewel of a mansion. We'd scamper from one stunning room to the next till we discovered our honeymoon suite. With gorgeous views of the ocean and crackling logs burning in the fireplace, we'd jump up into our four-poster bed and make mad passionate love. Then, as the sun is setting we'd stroll down the beach hand-in-hand and run back to the house and make love again. Too tired to cook from all the mind-blowing sex, we'd go out to a five star restaurant offering us sinfully delicious taste treats and we'd drink their most expensive wine only to rush back to our love nest and go at it again.

Hey, I'm a romantic.

But when we arrived at the house by the sea instead of a Victorian jewel we found a rundown 1980s timeshare condo, ten blocks from the ocean and ten thousand light years away from being romantic.

And I wouldn't say we scampered from room to room. Instead, we tripped, since there were only three; a living room and two bedrooms and all were horribly cluttered. And visions of hopping up into our honeymoon bed decked out in 1500 thread count sumptuous Egyptian sheets were squashed when we were put up in the children's bedroom with two twin beds fitted with broken-in rubber sheets.

A warm fire? They had no fireplace. But you advised me not to criticise too quickly when you noticed on our way to the gourmet restaurant, TGI Friday, that someone had set ablaze a trashcan on the street. How dreamy.

Walks on the beach? Sure, but we had to dodge in and out the pilings supporting the smoking oil refinery burping out sludge onto the sand.

And 'power gays'? I found out they are the most talented, successful and financially rewarded A-list gay men. Being a housecleaner and a dog groomer, I think Todd and Glenn are more like 'power poofs'. And their stories of being addicted to heroin and then finding Jesus and now adopting children horrified me. I haven't a maternal bone in my body but I was extremely concerned, after we polished off their box of wine, when Todd confessed to me that the Russian kid was missing a finger and he was going to send it back. The kid, that is.

Well, I took your advice and went out onto their tiny cement balcony to get some fresh air and enjoy the parking lot but failed to find a single star in the night sky due to massive amounts of pollution. It was then that you joined me and I immediately fell to my knees. No, I wasn't feeling amorous. Actually I thought you had stabbed me in the back.

Thank you Henry for rushing me back to the city and waiting patiently in the emergency room while they did a CAT scan of my pelvic floor. Who knew nine giant kidney stones growing in my two little kidneys could be such a blessing?

Plan A, the doctors wanted to flush the stones out with IV fluids but it was a teaching hospital and I was awarded the one student who had never inserted a shunt into a 'human' arm before. I was so grateful when you took over and showed him a thing or two. What are you, a closeted phlebotomist or a junkie? Don't answer that.

Plan B, I took your advice and tried your home remedy for dissolving kidney stones; six cans of cola consumed in two hours followed by one pound of raw asparagus juice then holding my bladder for as long as I could while doing a headstand. I did and promptly threw up, upside down while wetting my pants.

Plan C was shock wave therapy; bombarding my stones with 3000 zaps of acoustical sound. But of course my rocks were made of kryptonite and the shock didn't shake a thing.

So on to plan D. The doctor explained to us that he would slide a scope into my penis and travel through my bladder, on up to my ureter and then carefully lazar the stones, all while I was awake. Barely able to breath at the thought of this medieval torture device, you mortified me with what you said next.

"Hey Doc, I know people who enjoy the sensation of metal objects slipping into their wieners."

"Yes," the doctor said expressionless. "Those are sounds, hence we call it sounding."

"Some guys shove pens and plastic chopsticks in there," you added eagerly, "but I prefer spit and a thermometer. I like to see how hot I can get."

Hot? Personally, I found the subject so revolting that I started retching violently. And lo and behold, due to the extreme spasms and contortions of my body, I dislodged and birthed my nine little babies all on my own.

Henry I'm not judging you, but you're a freak. Don't contact me, again. And if you insist on stuffing yourself with inanimate objects, please use the mercury filled glassed thermometer for taking temperature IN YOUR MOUTH ONLY and go to the local sex shop and buy yourself a tub of lube and a safe stainless steel rod.

That's just sound advice.

All the best,
Arthur

MACRONEUROTIC

January/February 2009

Dear Henry,

I'm concerned that you took what I said in my last letter seriously. Well, I was serious about everything except the part about you being responsible for dislodging the nine walnut sized kidney stones from my ureter. In truth, it was a combination of drinking four liters of lemon water every day plus the help of all the gods I prayed to that allowed my self-made calcium oxalate rocks to tumble down into my bladder before tearing their way out through my urethra.

Hence, I was quite confused if not alarmed when I received your new business card in the mail. It read:

HENRY BRIMBLECUM
Healer-At-Large
reiki master – shiatsu practitioner – reflexologist
tarot reader – rolfer – acupuncturist
past life regressionist – high colonic irrigationist
collector of vinyl

Henry, I passed my stones just three weeks ago? I find it hard to believe that you could have mastered all these modalities in so little time. But my friends are always nagging at me not to judge too quickly, so I booked an appointment with you.

I understand your desire to create a Zen atmosphere in your apartment however throwing everything out but your skanky futon doesn't equal tranquility. And when I questioned you about the contraband you were burning there was no need to get so defensive. I didn't know that igniting sage cleanses the air of negative energy. Breathe deep, dear. It smelled an awful lot like pot.

But I forced myself to keep an open mind and allowed you to do some bodywork on me. Honestly, my lower back was still wound up in knots after birthing those boulders so a little shatzy, um shitsu, oops shiseido, I mean shiatsu sounded fantastic. But the session was over before it began and I missed out on my happy ending just because I made the comment about your hands being cold and clammy. I think you need to develop a thicker and drier skin if you're going to be a healer.

Next was past life regression. You had me count backwards from 100 very slowly and I'm sorry that it took me till number four to go "under" but I didn't want to fake it. And how was I to know that in 724 B.C. I was known as Pythia working my magic at Delphi in Greece? It's not like I asked to be the oracle, so no need to be jealous. Hey, it was a tough job being high priestess but someone had to do it. And speaking of high, I was smashed on hydrocarbon gases that were escaping up from cracks in the earth, which induced me into euphoric and excited if not incoherent conversations followed by amnesia. Hmmm, some things never change.

I picked up your business card and reread the part about you being a 'collector of vinyl'. I just assumed this meant you were buying up old records, which is pretty hip. So when you brought out your collection of vinyl clothing I had to laugh. That clear pantsuit made you look like a walking condom.

And it was lovely that you planned a meal for us but becoming an absolute macrobiotic overnight is a bit extreme. I'm a huge foodie. In fact, I think I'm a fat man trapped in a thin body. I'll eat anything (no comment) but your menu did seem a bit daunting. I understand that macrobiotics choose natural foods that are unprocessed and balance out the yin and the yang qualities. I'm all for eating healthy but I think you need to take some cooking classes.

You served me Peas Porridge Cold! Darling, I know the nursery rhyme and that some like it hot and others like it in the pot nine days old but I think you left yours in the saucepan for about a month. I dipped my spoon in and the entire bowlful of peas came out in one clump. And as yummy as they sounded I skipped your mock fish balls, kukicha tea and boiled Russian kale and unfortunately dove right into the no-meat loaf. It was made up of tempeh with 'special' bacteria (I don't want to know) and seitan (wheat gluten) that bound it all together. Yeah, it made it as hard as your porridge and after taking one bite I promptly chipped my front tooth.

My clear judgment obviously impaired by the mind numbing pain, I allowed you to practice your newly mastered art of acupuncture on my suffering body. Actually, it was so intense when you jammed that needle into the very top of my skull that my tooth stopped throbbing. That is until you inserted the next needle into the carotid artery in my neck and from then on the emergency medical crew had to take over. Even Sebastian Horsley – the

46

self-proclaimed modern day dandy who crucified himself – would have objected.

My dear friend, during the past year that we have been dating, you have vacillated from one fad and fetish to the next. You made love to my tassel loafers, ate only white food for two months and then pierced your member with a gigantic titanium barbell Prince Albert. You were an accountant who gained three stone, transformed into a trannie wearing Spanx, tried to non-surgically restore my foreskin and attempted to bleach my brown eye. You had my name (spelled incorrectly) tattooed onto you as a tramp stamp and were found hog-tied naked in the park high on crystal meth, which charmingly landed you in the slammer. You hot waxed off my left nipple, became a Scientologist and then admitted that you enjoy slipping anything you can get your hands on, into your penis. That one still makes me weak in the knees.

Henry, you're a macroneurotic negative new age junkie who is a detriment to society. Our love affair is over. Due to a court order you are forbidden to call, email, text or even see me in person. My lawyers and doctors fear for my life.

Happy Holiday and all the best,
Arthur

ARE YOU AN INNY OR AN OUTTY?

March/April 2009

Dear Henry,

I should have written sooner to thank you for my birthday present but truth be told you had the wrong day and the wrong month. And you sent it to the wrong address. You're an ass. But my mum always taught me to be polite so...thank you. And thank you for the homemade card. I thought the photograph of that magnificent naked man lying on the raft in that stunning pool was tastefully erotic until I realised it was me! You took that picture without me knowing it when we visited my friend Jon's house in the country. What are you, an undercover paparazzi? And now it's all over the internet. I went to your profile on the chat site we first met at and there is my naked bum up as your main profile pic and you're telling everyone it's you. Take my picture down now or I'm taking you up on charges and you'll be heading back to jail and sharing a cell with Boy George.

But like I said, I was taught to be polite. So thank you for the lottery ticket that was inside my birthday card. Normally when I buy a ticket I watch with baited breath to see if I won but since this drawing had already passed, I actually forgot about it till I was cleaning up my desk. Feeling very blasé and unexcited about the results I was shocked to discover that I won that Saturday's draw in the National Lottery and took a deep breath before reporting my winning of ... 1.9 million pounds! I certainly haven't been hurting financially but Henry, now I'm rich! And considering you're so poor you're beyond bankruptcy I thought it only fair that I share some of my windfall with you.

I admit that I was initially nervous when I discovered that you sank every cent I gave you into one investment. But ultimately I was impressed that your choice was the very new and successful gay gym/sauna/bar in Soho called Sweatgland. Man that's one exclusive club. I swear that when I walked through that metal detector at the front door it was measuring my muscle mass to see if I qualified to enter. I work out and yes, the guys at my gym have nicknamed me Buffy but next to these chiseled slabs of beef I looked like Amy Winehouse.

The place was full of one stud after another buddying up to work out with each other wearing the skimpiest of loincloths. I quickly changed into my gym clothes. But realising that wearing shorts and a tank top made me way overdressed, I tore off the shirt and claimed the only space left in the weight lifting section. However, there were no available weights. So instead I started doing intense squat thrusts. I stood with my feet together and squatted down. I placed my hands on the floor next to my feet and in an explosive movement I jumped backwards into a push-up position. But little did I know that a South American beauty was standing directly behind me. He was so sexy and so oiled up that we both fell to the floor with him slipping on top of me. "Damn," I thought to myself, "now we're gonna have to get married." Sweat from anticipation (not from working out) clouded my vision and I couldn't tell if the other members were lifting weights or having sex. Or maybe both?

Quickly I wormed away from my bride-to-be and decided I had to check out the sauna downstairs if only to make sure that you made a good investment. I dashed to my locker, stripped down naked and then cautiously slithered amongst the labyrinth of tunnels, play cabins and happy ending massage rooms. Suddenly I stumbled upon the 50 man Ibiza style foam party steam room decked out with a gigantic cannon in the shape of a penis which was spurting out copious amounts of soap bubbles. Call me madcap but I don't find tripping through a maze of tangled bodies in a sea of blinding suds…hot. Well, my eyes did. They were bloody stinging. And correct me if I'm wrong but doesn't everyone in your gym seem to be Brazilian? I mean they're gorgeous and all but I'm an equal opportunity fruit picker. I like all types of men and nationalities. Is the point of disembarkation from Rio to London at the entrance to Sweatgland?

Considering how well you invested your share of the fortune, I listened to my gut feelings and then promptly ignored them and allowed you to invest all my money in another venture. How talented of you to find the one and only Madoff type ponzi scheme still operating and sink everything I owned into it. Henry, I'm broke! This is the last straw. No more phone calls. No more dinners. No more sex. No more you. I'm through with men!

Instead of jumping off a bridge I ran over to Polari, the gay literary salon held over at Freedom Bar and was relieved to run into my friends Clayton Littlewood and Paul Burston. Without a pound in my pants the boys offered to buy a plethora of drinks and just before Clay was to read from his book *Dirty White Boy: Tales Of Soho*, lo and behold, you show up drunk. Everyone thought you were the 'warm-up act' as you stumbled onto the stage. Fortunately you were totally incoherent except for the part where you screamed out to the audience that I was a nasty old queen who is now straight. What the hell are you talking about? I'm so out, I was born gay. I was a breach. I came out ass first! I'm not switching teams at this point in my life. I'm just over you.

Honestly Henry, it's a sad day when a scorned lover tries to 'in' you.

All the best,
Arthur

FULL DISCLOSURE

May/June 2009

Dear Henry,

Truly, you are the last person on earth I thought I'd ever want to speak to again after you lost all my money in that ponzi like investment scheme. But when I discovered that you had quadrupled the money you sank into the Sweat-gland gym/sauna/bar in Soho and then turned around and offered to share half of it with me, I was stunned. It reminded me that in relationships it's important to be honest, upfront and forgiving; so when you offered to treat me to a classy and romantic 'make-up' dinner how could I say no? But the Stock Pot on Old Compton Street?

Without wasting a moment you sat me down, grabbed my hand and started in on your spiel…

Arthur, this is a story about my first true love and me. No one knows this happened and I must tell you about it or I don't think I can go on with our relationship. I had a couple of hot dates but no sex yet with the hunkiest man I'd ever met in my life. He invited me over to his flat and I was so thrilled that we were finally going to do 'it' that as I was ringing his doorbell I realised I had to go to the bathroom. He answered the door dressed in hot spandex and had candles lit and a bottle of Chianti open. Even more excited, I thought if I don't get to the bathroom now, I'll shit in my pants. And just then he tells me to relax, have some wine and he'll be right out of the bathroom.

Well, I panicked. Holding my hand to my butt I ran into the kitchen looking for a garbage bag but couldn't find one. I couldn't even locate the trashcan. Desperate, I ran into his bedroom and saw a plastic tub full of dirt. So I dropped my pants and pooped into his litter box. I grabbed some tissue, wiped and threw it into the box and then covered it with a pillow and rushed into the living room just as he was coming out of the bathroom. Suspicious, he looked at me and then walked into the bedroom. I put my hands to my mouth not knowing what was going to happen next.

"Henry, you Goddamn freaking girl cock!" he said, as he came into the living room holding his nose and carrying the litter box with the pillow over it. "Do you mind explaining this to me?"

"Uh, your cat took a big dump?"

"I don't have a cat."

"What?"

"And you just ruined my brand new ergonomic neck pillow."

"But…"

"You shat in my newly planted flower box and owe me 70 pounds for the pillow." He wrestled all the money I had out of my pocket and then opened the door. "It's over pussy boy. Get out!"

Henry, I thought you couldn't see me laughing because you were crying so hard. Angry and hurt, you insisted that I share with you the story of my first true love. You asked for it.

At age 13 I must have been hormonally retarded because I still didn't know how a woman got pregnant. Yes, I understood biologically but I just didn't know how the sperm came out. I thought maybe the man pees into the woman?

Well, one blistering summer day when my mother was out doing errands I blew up a pool raft. You know the kind that had holes on the side so you could sip a glass and rest it while floating in water? I stripped down naked, lathered my body up with baby oil and laid down in the thing out on the grass. Suddenly, my mum came home and started hollering for me. I jumped up, slid on the raft, lost my balance and fell back onto it with my talliwacker sliding right into the tight warm hole meant for a tall cool drink. I found out instantly how the sperm comes out of the man.

I named the raft Ken and fell madly in love with it. The two of us were inseparable. Going at it three, four, even five times a day. I was making up for lost time. Boy, I had such a great tan that summer. But one day when I was rushing home to rendezvous with Ken, I discovered my mum burning something in the backyard.

"Arthur, stay away! Don't breathe the air."

"Mother, what are you doing?"

"That raft stunk to high heaven. Whatever was all over that thing, I'll never know. Must have been bacteria. I had to torch it."

I can't tell you how brokenhearted I was the day I found out that my mum had murdered Ken. She burned him at the stake, just like Joan of Arc.

After a proper mourning period, I did set out to meet new friends. I had a tight but risky relationship with the cushions on the sofa. They were covered in plastic, so clean up was a breeze. But family members had an annoying habit of walking in on us. One day my older sister Kelly caught us in a passionate interlude.

"Mother, Arthur is humping the couch again! You are such a disgusting pervert. I am never sitting on that thing, again."

She turned on the television and sat down in the recliner, not knowing that we, too, had recently met and fallen in love.

And finally, one day I did discover my right hand. And to spice things up I would switch to the left and pretend it was a stranger. But it's Ken for whom I will always hold a special place in my heart.

Henry, you forced this confession out of me and now I realise why you'll never be enough man for me. Goodbye and good luck. I understand if you feel jealous but it's never a good idea to share everything from your past with a boyfriend.

I loved that raft. I loved Ken unconditionally.

All the best,
Arthur

THERE'S THE RUB-BER

August/September 2009

Dear Henry,

Two friends of mine who have been in a long-term relationship shared with me how they've managed to stay in love all this time and not kill each other. Their advice? Keep an open mind.

The last time we were together I shared with you my true feelings for Ken, the raft. Many men would have run when they discovered I had a meaningful relationship with a plastic flotation device early on in life, but not you. You said it brought us closer. Henry, you surprise me at every turn.

Therefore I was grateful you accepted my apology and eager to see you once more. And intrigued by the box and invitation you had sent over to my flat. The note said I was to meet you at a mysterious location to celebrate our making-up and enclosed was a special outfit I had to wear. Inside I found a rubber lace-up sleeveless top, a rubber jock and a gas mask. I was confused, apprehensive and fascinated. I put the items on, then a pair of pants and shirt over them and slipped on a pair of Wellies cause it was supposed to rain. I took a large breath and an even larger Klonopin, pulled out the directions, grabbed my gas mask and headed out the door.

As instructed I took a taxi to a dilapidated brick warehouse where a humongous man dressed in black rubber from head to toe was guarding a rusty metal door.

"Itsy?" I asked very tentatively.

He grunted, "Yeah, but you can't go in like that."

"Oh, I have on my outfit on underneath."

So he ordered me to take my shirt and pants off. I looked both ways and seeing no one, I quickly stripped down standing there in my rubber garb, my Wellies and held my gas mask in my hand. I grabbed my wallet and keys and shoved them into a zipper pouch in my shirt as he took my clothes. He slid the heavy door to the side revealing a big sign that read, "International Association Of Rubberists Honor Fetish."

"Put your mask on," he barked as he slammed the door shut behind me.

But before I had a chance to I was assaulted by copious amounts of stage smoke, which triggered off a convulsive coughing fit. Once I got the mask on I felt my way down a dark hallway as some sort of techno music got louder and louder. I stood before a massive mirror and strained to recognize the image staring back at me. I looked like a giant fly. A giant rubber fly in a jock and Wellies.

I stumbled my way into a cavernous room and found myself standing next to scores of people wearing all sorts of bizarre rubber outfits watching a person standing on an alter. He was zipped up in a latex body bag and was rubbing himself up and down giant religious artifacts. A plaque on the alter read, "Hierophiliac".

"Henry?"

A sea of buggy looking rubbers looked back at me as I walked on. Another crowd was looking down into a pit that had a huge clear plastic bag in it. And inside the bag was a man breathing through a small tube. A machine kicked on, sucking the air out of the bag. Then a hooded and extremely hairy bear wearing a rubber thong jumped into the pit and started rolling all over the vacuum packed person. A plaque on the pit read, "Hirsutophiliac".

"Henry?"

I walked on and found myself in a large room full of more rubbers standing in a circle staring up at someone trapped in an elevated bondage cage wearing a bright purple straight jacket, matching hood and no pants.

"Henry?"

A plaque on the cell read, "Urophiliac". I thought to myself, "Isn't that a…" and just at that moment a golden shower sprayed over all of us.

Stunned, blinded and wishing my mask had windshield wipers I groped my way to a giant water tank. People were watching someone in an inflated catsuit with attached gloves, feet and hood floating effortlessly on their back. You unzipped your mouthpiece and pointed at me.

"He's the kenophiliac!"

The crowd turned to me as I took off my gas mask and you laboriously flipped over onto your stomach. You unzipped the rear of your suit and started pointing to it, as was the rest of the crowd. That's when I noticed the two plaques on your water tank that read, "Eproctophiliac" and "Kenophiliac". The crowd started cheering and pumping their arms and that's when I panicked. They picked me up and threw me into the tank. Suddenly, hundreds of bubbles appeared in the water. Your flatulent stench was so bad but familiar that I suddenly knew what an eproctophiliac was. Thank God I had my gas mask. I slipped it back on and desperately pulled myself out of the tank and ran.

When I got to the giant metal door a small rubber person offered me a plastic raincoat.

"Where's Itsy?" I screamed.

"Gone. It's raining."

I looked back and rubbers were coming after me so I grabbed the coat, slid open the heavy metal door and took off. Without a taxi in sight I hunted for the tube and once safe and secure underground I realised that the raincoat I had on was clear and see-through. So I rode all the way home wearing my rubber sleeveless shirt, Wellies, rubber jock strap and gas mask. Well almost all the way. I was arrested one stop from my flat for indecent exposure.

Henry, I am neither an exhibitionist nor a voyeur and I'm certainly not attracted to eproctophiliacs. I do have an open mind and I appreciate your attempt to be my human Ken doll but your public display of affection was simply revolting. And thanks to you I now have a criminal record. Please do not contact me again. Ever!

All the best,
Arthur

SMILE! YOU'RE ON CANDID CAMMING!

November/December 2009

Dear Henry,

Although I never thought I'd speak to you again after our last disastrous rendezvous I am proud of myself that I was non-judgmental enough to explore your sick and twisted fixation with rubber. But thanks to you I now have a criminal record. It is considerate that you borrowed another rubberist's phone and tried calling me on my cell during the altercation with the police but how many times do I have to tell you that no one has reception in the tube?

It just confirms what I've been saying all along that communication is key in any relationship. Hence, I was surprised when a brand new iPhone was delivered to my house from you. And you bought yourself one, too. Welcome to the 21st century, Henry.

So, you are no longer attached to landline phones. You're the only person I know who was still making calls from public pay phones. Actually, when we first met didn't you send me smoke signals? Sorry, my bad. That's when you burnt down your apartment building.

I know it was hard for you to absorb and assimilate everything that the phone can do for you but once you figured out how to make phone calls there was no stop-ping you. Day and night you were calling me with urgent, dire, calamitous, important, life threatening messages.

"Arthur? It's me, Henry. I'm on my way to the store to get kitty litter. I love my new feral cat and want her to have the best things in life. Organic chicken and basmati rice for my pussy tonight. Arthur? Arthur, can you hear me? Can you hear…" Click.

One thing I miss with cell phones is that you can't SLAM them down!

And when it came time to show you how to send emails from your phone I was shocked to discover that you didn't even have an Internet account with any server. But as soon as you were set up I started receiving mes-sages from a certain…

ffwspigslutsubbttmin2cbt4anonymousLRT@yahoo.com

…so it only makes sense that I blocked you as spam. You can't be sending out an embarrassing address like that – everyone knows it's LTR not LRT.

Then I cursed myself for showing you how to send text messages.

3:59 am BLEEP "arthur…my kitty is walking all… bowlegged"

4:45 am BLEEP "arthur…my kitty hasn't gone in a week…o u know how 2 relieve anal gland impaction?"

5:30 am BLEEP "arthur…i figured it out…just had 2 massage her anal sac with my thumbs…all is ex-pressed…did u know that's what they spray when they mark something?… want 2 come over 4 breakfast?"

Henry, I don't have an unlimited plan so every time

you send a text I'm charged for it. Stop it! God forgive me, I've created a monster.

But someone else has to take credit for showing you how to set up a Facebook page. This site was cool for ten seconds while everyone was still on Mybook...I mean Spaceface...uh...Myspace. You're not only late for the party but the only person I know who had their profile deleted due to offensive material. What were you posting? And people on these sites use their real names not handles like yours - Dusty Boots.

Facebook Status Update: Dusty Boots 1:30 am "beef-eater...luv meetin u at the Fur Ball...arthur's mad at me so im sure im single...AGAIN...lol...cum over..." 3 minutes ago.

You obviously have your Facebook and Twitter accounts connected. Your Tweets show up as your status updates. That's annoying! And yes, I am mad at you, AGAIN.

So it was a total surprise when I got an instant message from you on yahoo asking my permission to accept your video cam. After minutes of you begging I made the big mistake of allowing you to appear. You were nude and aroused, no surprise. But as your cam panned up your body I had to strain to see what was attached to your face. Now I'm not the hippest person in the world but I think I've heard of most 'sexual devices' but this is the first time I had seen this. You were wearing a clear plastic mask over your nose and mouth and it seemed as though a bottle of poppers was attached to it. A popper mask?

I didn't even click off my cam. I rushed out of my apartment and over to yours, not because I was overcome with sexual excitement...I was horrified. Henry, that stuff kills brain cells. That's why it feels so good.

But when you opened your door you were holding the mask in your hand and laughing.

"Arthur, I knew this would get you over here. It's empty, no poppers."

Relieved and still baffled by your bizarre sense of humor I listened to my gut instincts and then promptly ignored them and allowed you to make love to me. Several times over. And I must admit, it was fantastic. That is until I dragged myself home and opened an email from a close friend.

"Arthur, dude! Do you know that there is a camming session of you having sex posted on xtube? That new diet is paying off. Hot!"

I didn't know you were capturing us! And you posted it on xtube? My face is showing! I sent a message to the site and they said they're not responsible for the content and you have to remove the post. Do it now Henry or I'll have you arrested! And get flattering lighting.

I'm sorry I ever introduced you to the world of communication. You're irresponsible and a detriment to society. Don't call, email, Myspace, Facebook, cam, instant message or Tweet me! Ever.

All the best,
Arthur

CRUISING FOR A BRUISING

January/February 2010

Dear Henry,

I'm writing this letter to calm myself down and try to make some sort of sense out of the chaotic moments that led up to the shocking end of our gay cruise together.

Yes, I was furious at you when I discovered that you had posted a vid of us having sex on xtube but all was forgiven when you decided to treat me to a one-week vacation to the Western Caribbean. The thought of floating through the seas trapped on a ship filled with 3,700 queens has always filled me with great trepidation but hey, I like to live dangerously. I never thought anyone ever won those online sweepstakes but Henry, I'm sure glad you proved me wrong.

Call me madcap but I think flying is romantic. I love shaky takeoffs where you just know the plane isn't going fast enough or harrowing landings where runways are too short and we're all thrown forward while the pilot slams on the brakes. Hence, I was looking forward to experiencing it with you but unfortunately you don't share my passion for the friendly skies. Instead you swallowed a triple dose of Valium and chased it with a bottle of cheap champagne and promptly passed out. So I basically flew the long, lonely flight to Ft. Lauderdale, Florida by myself.

Unfortunately we couldn't enjoy this seaside gay Mecca because from the moment we landed till the time we boarded the ship, torrential downpours and exfoliating whipping sand dampened everyone's spirits. But our extremely spacious one bedroom Queen's Suite (appropriately named) with oversized balcony on the ship was stunning. But it was annoyingly located on deck eleven. And on deck twelve was the main restaurant. All night, every night, the grinding of dishwashers (the machines, not the men) working overtime made it absolutely impossible to sleep. So we joined everyone else on board and dragged our sorry asses up to the clubs and grinded our hips till the sun came up.

But why, during the entire trip, did they repeatedly blare this announcement?

"Experience Christopher Street, the world's only indoor gay street at sea, filled with shops, cafes and inviting bars. There's nothing quite like it anywhere."

That's right, there isn't. They had transformed the main lobby into their version of what this historic street used to be like 30 years ago in New York City's Greenwich Village. But little do they know that Christopher Street is now about as gay as Dagenham High Street!

I dreaded eating at a designated table full of strangers in the main restaurant so I was thrilled to discover that every gay man at ours was opting for liquid dinners. Sadly, so were you. Each night I sat there all by myself at a table set for ten while a captain, two waiters and three busboys hovered about my every move as I ate my way through the Caribbean.

The ports of call were surprisingly fantastic. From Cozumel and the gorgeous Mayan ruins in Tulum to the plethora of frightening stingrays in the Grand Cayman Islands to tropical river tubing with gorgeous local boys in Jamaica. But I found it frustrating, Henry, that you never left the ship. Wait, I take that back. In the Internet café you did find a hot guy in Jamaica to hook up with but narrowly escaped with your life when his wife came home with their thirteen children, one goat and a four-foot long machete.

And the entertainment? Predictable drag bingo, the newlywed game, the toga party, the semen and sailor's dance and bad awful karaoke. And while the program boasted past comedic performers the likes of Joan Rivers, Margaret Cho and Rosie O'Donnell, we got stuck with the only gay hypnotist in show business – Lance Trance. Henry, it was amusing to see you bark like a dog in Spanish but I've seen you do that numerous times after drinking lethal amounts of Absinthe and under the spell of the green fairy.

The pools were nice but the gorgeous gym rats being photographed for the next season's brochure made for an intimating atmosphere. And there were certainly plenty of physical activities to keep one busy but it was the one and only Patti LuPone that I was saving my energy up for.

Scheduled to perform on the last night of the cruise, we were all heartbroken when she opted to eat at the ship's sushi bar (seven day old raw fish?) and managed to contract the world's worst case of food poisoning. They airlifted her off the boat as a bevy of queens sang *Don't Cry For Us Broadway Diva* and the ship's clever staff came up with a comparable solution. Replacing her with the one and only Richard Simmons, the now anorexic but more obnoxious aerobics/diet guru. Force me to walk the plank now, please.

Speaking of which, it was while enjoying the ship's cantilevered whirlpool that sat 32 men and extended 112 feet out over the sea that everything came to a shocking end. Maybe it was the eighth Sex On The Beach you drank or the umpteen line of something you were snorting or possibly the intense swelling of ocean just at that inopportune moment but before we knew it, you were gone. You fell overboard. I knew you weren't enjoying the cruise but talk about drowning one's sorrows.

I was horrified, to say the least, but it was considerate that the captain circled the area once, looking for you. But I totally understood that it would be impolite and a bother to the other passengers if we were late for Key West. So off we went.

Henry, during the two years we dated you nearly killed me a dozen times over. But I have to admit it was never dull being your boyfriend. Normally I'd rant and rave about how I never ever want to speak to or see you again but now that you are gone…well, I fear I'm going to miss your shining face. Bon Voyage!

Rest In Peace and
All the best,
Arthur

OLD HALF

March/April 2010

Dear Henry,

After you fell overboard during our gay cruise to the Western Caribbean and were nowhere to be found, I toasted bon voyage and wished you well and tried to move on with my life. And I thought my last letter to you would bring closure to our relationship but surprisingly that was not the case. Back home, whenever I frequented one of your old haunts, it was your spirit that haunted me.

While sipping burnt coffee in your favorite restaurant, The Stockpot in Soho, I thought I saw you sitting across the room. But alas it was just the famous and larger than life madam, Sue, from Old Compton Street.

One day when running around town thinking my bladder was about to burst I scooted into the public lavatory in Pond Square and swear I saw you cottaging in the back stall. Wrong again. It was just a homeless Ena Sharples setting up tent.

And when I found myself overworked and stressed out one sleepless night and decided to connect with a complete stranger on your favorite website, eroticmassage-partner.com, I knew his rough and scaly hands caused by ichthyosis vulgaris were yours. That is until he took off the loofah mitts. But nagging thoughts of you permeated my dreams as I drifted off to Pluto and back again just in time for my happy ending.

Like a bad rash Henry, you just wouldn't go away. So I decided to ignore every healthy and self-protective instinct I had in my body and I called your family.

It was your mum who answered the phone declaring that her name was Domina the Dictress and asked if I was interested in the three-hour reduced special. Henry, you never told me she was a dominatrix.

I explained who I was and she immediately shifted into mother mode saying my timing was perfect. The whole family was about to celebrate your short-lived life with a memorial. She insisted I meet up with her right away at your home address and warned me not to be late.

Sensing she wasn't just any old kitten with a whip, I obeyed her orders sped over to her flat pronto. She answered the door decked out in a shiny latex catsuit, thigh high leather boots and extension-laden hair piled high upon her head. With her whip in one hand and a male lover in the other (where is your father?) who was clad only in a black leather thong and dog collar, she barked at both of us to jump into a waiting taxi.

Our foreign driver who spoke every language except English and obviously graduated from Whiplash Auto School careened dangerously through the streets of the city as the man/dog sat there licking her boots and I gripped my fastened seatbelt with white knuckles.

She had the taxi come to a screeching halt in front of …Chariots?

We poured out of the car and looked up at the massive complex, which boasted having the largest sauna in London. The man/dog and I followed your mum as she scoured the swimming pool, the work-out gym, the 12

69

massage rooms, the 500 locker changing room, the 2 giant steam rooms, a plethora of octogenarians, the 50 resting rooms, the 3 Jacuzzis and finally discovered what she was looking for in the internet café. Her husband, your father, with a gigantic German shepherd seeing-eye dog. Henry, you never told me he was blind?

She shouted at him and pointed across the room. "Why the hell are you scouring Gaydar online when there's sex on tap right there in the 30 man steam room?"

Gaydar? And how could he be online and blind at the same time? He must have one of those computer voice generated programs. She snapped her whip, spun around on her dangerously high and spiked heels and signaled her husband, his seeing-eye dog, her man/dog and I, to follow her down a dark labyrinth of hallways. "I know he's in here," she insisted.

Suddenly she stopped in front of the video lounge, put her hand to her heart and smiled proudly. Meanwhile, we, the three stooges and their seeing-eye dog, ungracefully collided into each other. Domina stretched out both arms towards him and then shocker of all shockers, she shed a tear.

It was your nineteen-year-old brother, Clark. And he was standing on a makeshift coffee table stage singing, *Cry Me A River* into an extremely large, black...dildo? As he ended his torch song, a few listeners woke up and applauded as Domina rushed to his side.

"Baby, I'm so thrilled you're enjoying your birthday present," she purred as she stroked the enormous black shaft he was gripping and then pulled him out of the club followed by her dog, your dad, his dog and me.

Stuffing ourselves into yet another taxi, we barreled

across town as your mother looked at her watch. "Driver, we're going to Last Resort Cabaret and make it snappy!" she screamed. "The memorial has already started."

Once inside the Last Resort (and trust me it was) we scrambled to find seats in the jam-packed lounge. On stage was a young man, a hip-hop dancer who was frighteningly flexible and was ending his routine by intentionally dislocating both his shoulders while doing the 'worm'. He jumped to his feet, relocated his armpits and ran off stage as the crowd applauded.

The announcer then told us that the next performer celebrating the short yet colorful life of Henry Brimblecum was the postmenopausal Japanese sensation, Rose Asia. Out shuffled the most exquisite woman dressed in a traditional kimono. She demurely stood before the microphone and the moment she opened her mouth to sing *I Enjoy Being A Girl* all of our ears perked up including your father's seeing-eye dog. She sang a bit more when suddenly the German shepherd went ballistic, charging towards the woman on stage. He recognized your voice.

Henry, she was...YOU!

We all ran up on stage drenched in tears, your father leading the way. That's when I discovered he wasn't blind, he was just wearing sunglasses. Why the dog? Well, your teenage brother whispered to me that your dad was experiencing 'k9' love. I don't want to know.

It turns out that you survived falling over board into the Gulf of Mexico and were picked up by an Asian trolling vessel. You had endured extreme mutilation to your body and suffered from amnesia. And once in Tokyo and the doctors examined you, they determined that you must be a woman and then set forth with extensive full body reconstruction.

Henry, you're gorgeous and I wish you well in your new body but I'm sorry, this will never work. You'll have to go on with your life as a 'newhalf' without me. I want the 'oldhalf'.

All the best,
Arthur

ABOUT THE AUTHOR

Arthur Wooten is the author of the critically acclaimed novels *Birthday Pie, On Picking Fruit* and *Fruit Cocktail,* as well as the children's book, *Wise Bear William: A New Beginning.* Also a playwright, his works include the award winning *Birthday Pie,* which had its world premiere at the Waterfront Playhouse, Key West, FL. His one act plays, *Lily* and *The Lunch,* have been produced Off-Off Broadway. Arthur grew up in Andover, MA and now resides in New York City.